BRAZIL

Serra dos Órgãos
National Park

black-capped
capuchin monkey

Town of
Guapimirim

City of
Rio de Janeiro

ATLANTIC OCEAN

A TINY BROWN MONKEY ON THE BIG BLUE EARTH

To my own little monkey, Jesse, and to Christopher, whose
many talents go beyond swinging from branches.—T.C.

To Mauro and Marcelo, who grew up with me in that magical rain
forest, and Eloise. To Veronica Scott, obrigada!—L.N.P.

Text copyright © 2019 Tory Christie • Illustrations copyright © 2019 Luciana Navarro Powell

Published in 2019 by Amicus Ink, an imprint of Amicus • P.O. Box 1329 • Mankato, MN 56002 • www.amicuspublishing.us

Library of Congress Cataloging-in-Publication Data
Names: Christie, Tory, author. | Powell, Luciana Navarro, illustrator.
Title: A tiny brown monkey on the big blue Earth / by Tory Christie ; illustrated by Luciana Navarro Powell.
Description: Mankato, Minnesota : Amicus Ink, [2019] | Summary: Illustrations and easy-to-read text show that a tiny monkey in
South America is in a jungle that is in a country on a continent on the Earth.
Identifiers: LCCN 2018048705 (print) | LCCN 2018052966 (ebook) | ISBN 9781681525204 (eBook) | ISBN 9781681524986 (hardcover)
Subjects: | CYAC: Perspective (Philosophy)--Fiction.
Classification: LCC PZ7.1.C546 (ebook) | LCC PZ7.1.C546 Tin 2019 (print) | DDC [E]--dc23
LC record available at https://lccn.loc.gov/2018048705

Editor: Rebecca Glaser | Designer: Veronica Scott

First edition 9 8 7 6 5 4 3 2 1
Printed in China

A TINY BROWN MONKEY BIG ON THE BLUE EARTH

by Tory Christie

illustrated by Luciana Navarro Powell

amicus ink

Mankato, Minnesota

A tiny brown monkey

Swings from a branch

in a
tall,
tall
tree

Nestled in a damp,
dark jungle

On the side of a
mountain with
a trail curving

down,

down,

down

To a cozy little town,

Where a bus

packed with people

Rumbles down

a narrow highway

In a lush,
green
country

Toward a busy city

That sits on the edge

of a grand

continent

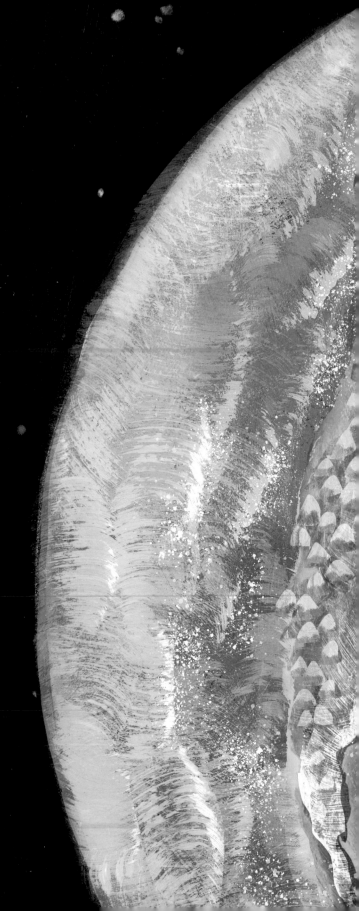

Surrounded
by an ocean

splash,

splash,

splashing

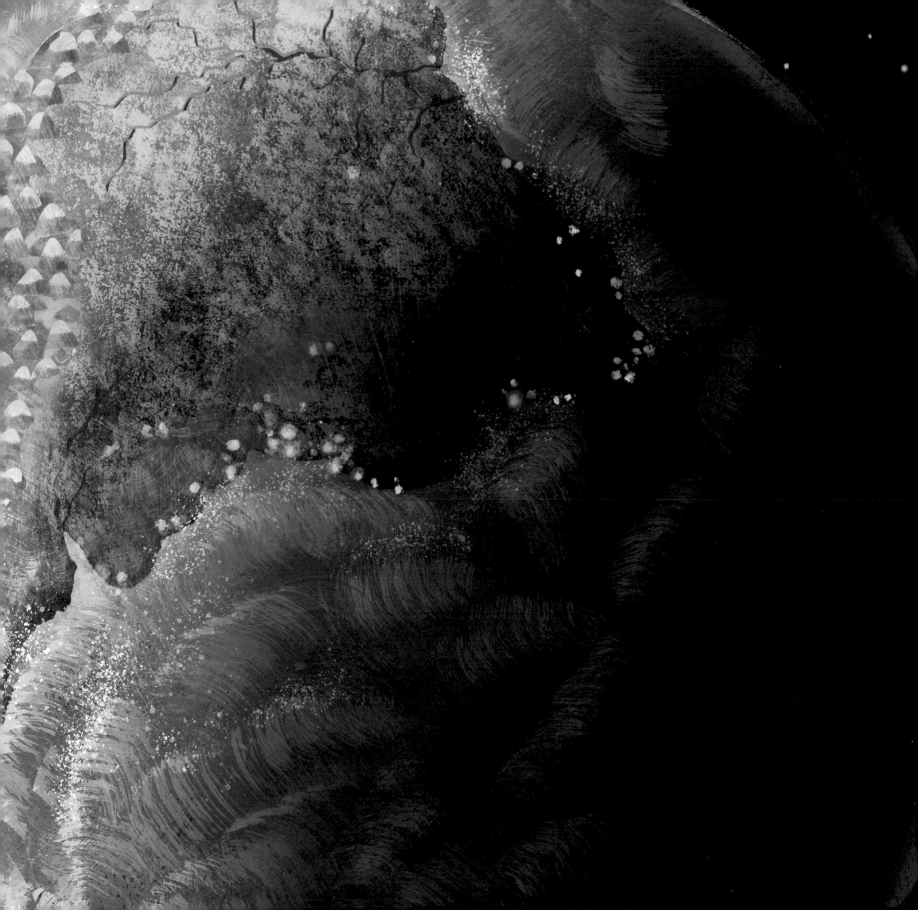

On the big blue Earth . . .

where a tiny
brown monkey

swings from
a branch.

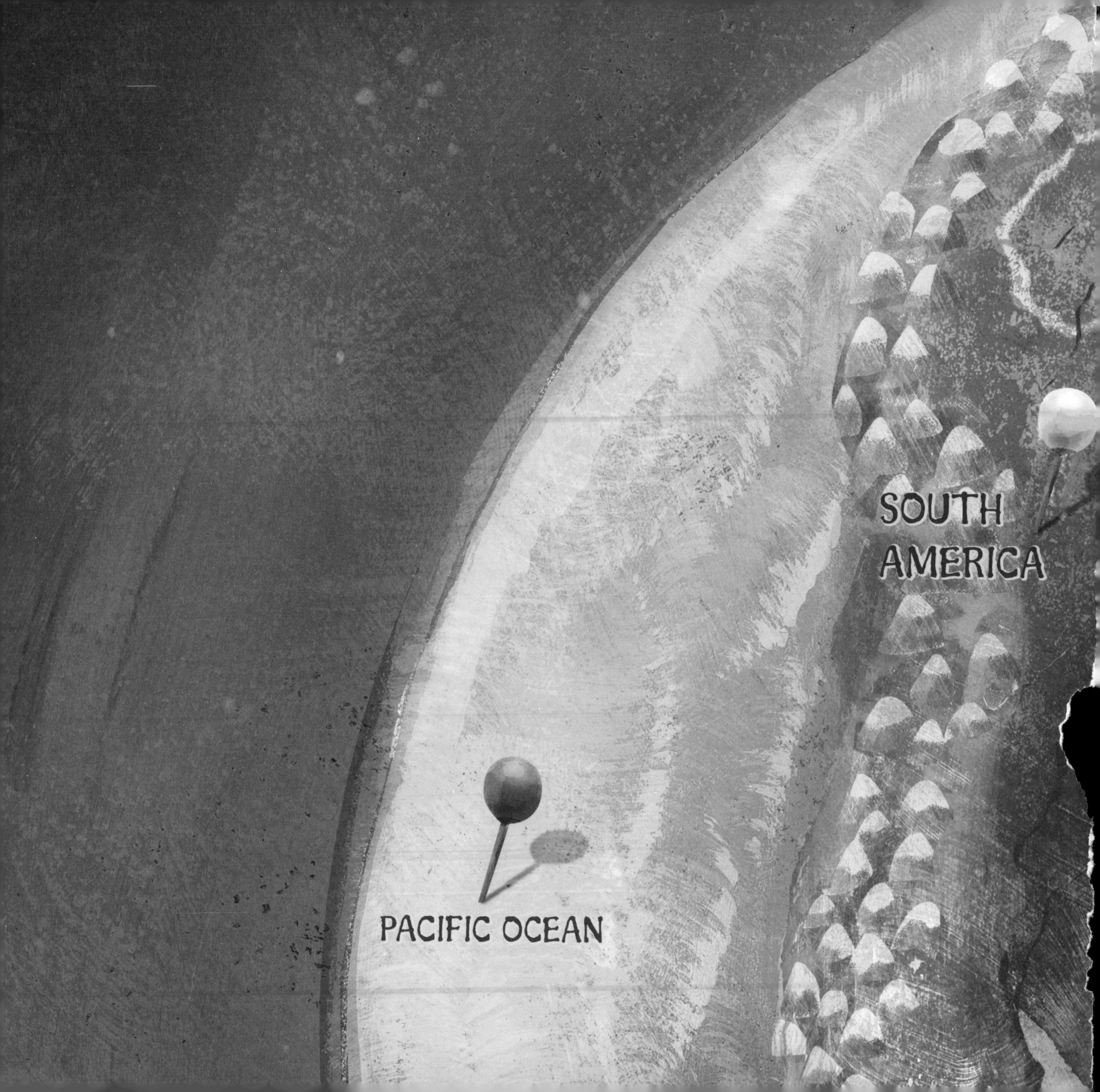
SOUTH
AMERICA
PACIFIC OCEAN